Memoirs
of a peasant boy

Xosé Neira Vilas

Publishing history
Original title: Memorias dun neno labrego © Copyright Xosé Neira Vilas
First published by Editorial Follas Novas, Buenos Aires, Argentina
1961.
Published by Ediciós do Castro, A Coruña, Spain, in 1968
Reprinted in 1969, 1971, 1972, 1976, 1977, 1979, 1980, 1981, 1982, 1984,
1985, 1986, 1989, 1991, 1993, 1995, 1996, 1999, 2001. (ISBN: 84-85134-
70-2).
Published by Ediciones Jucar, Madrid in 1974. Reprinted in 1979, 1985.
Published by Editorial Arte y Literatura, LA Havana, Cuba, 1977.
Published by Editorial Forja in Lisbon, Portugal, 1977.
Published by Editorial Gustav KiepenheuerVeralg, Leipzig, Germany,
1984.

Translation by Camilo Ogando Vázquez
© Copyright 2004 Camilo Ogando Vázquez. All rights reserved.

© Copyright 2004 Xosé Neira Vilas. All rights reserved.

Book design by Moyhill Publishing

Note for Librarians: a cataloguing record for this book that includes
Dewey Classification and US Library of Congress numbers is available
from the National Library of Canada. The complete cataloguing record
can be obtained from the National Library's online database at:
www.nlc-bnc.ca/amicus/index-e.html
ISBN 1-4120-2892-2

TRAFFORD
This book was published on-demand in cooperation with Trafford Publishing.
On-demand publishing is a unique process and service of making a book available for retail
sale to the public taking advantage of on-demand manufacturing and Internet marketing.
On-demand publishing includes promotions, retail sales, manufacturing, order fulfilment,
accounting and collecting royalties on behalf of the author.

Suite 6E, 2333 Government St., Victoria, B.C. V8T 4P4, CANADA
Phone 250-383-6864   Toll-free 1-888-232-4444 (Canada & US)
Fax 250-383-6804   E-mail sales@trafford.com   Web site www.trafford.com
TRAFFORD PUBLISHING IS A DIVISION OF TRAFFORD HOLDINGS LTD
Trafford Catalogue #04-0720   www.trafford.com/robots/04-0720.html

13   12   11   10   9   8   7   6   5   4   3

To Sergio, my son

A translation

by
Camilo Ogando Vázquez

Introduction

Galicia is a small community located on the northwest coast of Spain. Throughout history, this peripheral situation has made it isolated and poor, but also supported the development of its own language and culture, which has received the influence of the rest of Spain and Europe through the Route to Santiago, its capital city.

Its numerous mountains, hills, valleys, and rivers have shaped not only its countless small villages, but also the nature of its people: proud, tolerant, and understanding people who, despite their deep love for their own native soil, were forced to emigrate.

The novel you are about to read was first published in the Galician language in 1961 in Buenos Aires, Argentina, where the writer, like many other people at that time, had moved, escaping from the poverty and oppression in Spain.

The story takes place in Galicia in the 1930´s and 1940´s, when "poverty and drudgery in the fields had nested in our eyes," and is about a boy who, trying to flee from the repressed and stifling society he lives in, writes down everything that happens to him. In doing so, he criticizes the moral and social atmosphere. He also reflects the most essential social struggle, setting up the Galician language, spoken by the poor and oppressed, against Spanish, a foreign language for Balbino, "a boy from a village."

Since 1961, Memoirs of a peasant boy has become one of the most important novels in Galician literature. Moreover, it has been translated into several languages: Spanish, Catalan, Portuguese, Chinese, Russian, Czech, Italian, Bulgarian, and German.

I AM...

Balbino. A boy from a village. That's to say, a nobody. And worse, poor. Manolito[1] is from a village too, but he thinks he is superior to me in spite of what I did to him.

In summer, I go barefoot. The hot dust in the paths makes me stride. The grains of sand hurt me and there are always spikes sticking in my feet. I get up when night is still dark, at about two or three in the morning, to take the cattle to graze, to till, or to tie sheaves. By dawn, my back and my legs already ache. However, the day's work is still to be done. Thirst, heat, horseflies.

In winter, cold. Longing to be always by the fire. Closed watermills. Gossip about snow and wolves. Our arms are like racks for hanging rags. Red marks on my skin, injuries, numbed fingers.

---

[1]Manolito: is the landlord's son and is called Manolito (the Spanish name) instead of Manoliño (the Galician name). At that time, Galician was supposed to be spoken only by peasants.

What do town boys know about this?

They do not know what I think while I'm swallowing a sip of broth with corn bread. Or what I feel when I am on the moor, soaked and stiff, seeing misty ghosts in every tree.

The village is a mixture of mud and smoke, where dogs howl and people die "all in good time, "as my godmother would say. We boys are sad. We play, we run after fireworks and we even laugh, but we are sad. Poverty and drudgery in the fields have nested in our eyes.

I long to travel; to sail seas and visit other countries I don't know. I was born and brought up in the village, but now I feel it has become small and crowded. As if I was living in a beehive. I have thoughts I can tell no one. Some of them would never understand me, and others would call me a fool. That's why I write. And then I sleep like a dog. I'm relieved, free, as if I no longer carried the weight of a heavy load. That's me all over! But that's also Smith, the captain who fought in the war and when he went back home started to write about everything he had gone through. That's what is written in a book Landeiro brought me.

If only I could write a book! Not likely! I hope they won't find my notebook. I would be ashamed of it. It's worth all that - and more. Because I empty into it everything I feel. Few people do it.

Everybody opens their trap for two reasons: to tell the truth or to move away from it.

At home, they didn't understand me. And the same thing happens to me at Landeiro's. That's the worst thing a person can ever face, but many people never go through it.

I don't know if I talk nonsense. I see the world around me and long to understand it. I see shadows and lights, travelling storm clouds, fire, and trees. What are they, how do they happen? Nobody, for instance, tells me what stars are for, or where birds die. I know for sure that, long before I was born, the sun and rocks were already here and water flowed down the river. And I'm sure everything will be the same after I have died. More and more people will come, trampling on one another, deliberately forgetting those who have died, as if they had never lived.

Writing in the notebook – would you believe it? – is like emptying out my heart. It seems like a miracle. After all, it's nothing but a conversation with myself. But everything is a miracle to me: from drops of rain to the chirp of crickets.

Even if I thought of writing a book, as Smith did, what I'd tell would be worthless. Smith fought in the war and I am just "the boy," as they call me at home. I'm Balbino. A boy from a village. A nobody.

Memoirs of a peasant boy

LOST

"BOOOOOY!"

"Balbino!"

Those are the first calls I remember. My mother and Aunt Carme were striding along down the farmland. Their shouts struck the quarry on the other side of the river. Without heeding roads or paths, they ran freely, smashing the maize. It was just after lunch. The sun was beating down. Annoyed horseflies were buzzing.

"What might have happened to the boy?"

"Might he have fallen into the river?"

"God help us!"

The day before, my father had beaten me up because I had soiled the landlord's son with soot. A very clean boy, who eats white bread, drinks milk with coffee, and doesn't have to get up early to take the cattle to graze. My father didn't want to know what Manolito had done to me before.

"He's the landlord's son, and that's enough."

But much as he should be so, it seems to me that he has no right to kick me on the shins with his new shoes, or to spit at me, or to tell me that, if they want, we will have to leave the house and the land.

Furious as I was, I went to bed without having dinner and spent the night awake, weeping. I felt sorry for myself because I was a poor boy. Those completely poor who, wearing rags, beg, and sometimes even steal potatoes or maize to get something to eat, live better than me. They put up with other people, but not those of their own families who want to stand well with the landlord. Because they may have something to eat, or they may not, they may or may not have clogs, but they are rid of the landlord and of Manolito.

The morning after, I got up when they all did. I went to the moor with my father. He noticed I was upset, but he said nothing. And I made a wry face. We went back, without saying a word, when the oxen started to drive away the flies with their tails.

After having lunch, I went to the threshing-floor. Aunt Carme followed me, but when she saw I was lying in the shade, in the straw loft, she turned back. Then, I pushed the gate open, crossed the road, and headed for the farmland. I went on through the rows of maize. I was walking slowly. The maize was hiding me. They could no longer see me. The soil was hard. Some clods crumbled under my clogs. I walked on and on. I might be near the river because the din of the water in the dam, by the mill, came up to me.

I sat down. I took off my clogs and unbuttoned my shirt. I was tired and sleep overcame me. I slept for a good while, I don't know for how long, and, in my dreams, I fancied Manolito running after me with a shotgun.

"They may be looking for me," I thought. But I didn't care. My father had smacked me with no reason, and I wanted to show him I'm not scared. That's why I had run away. At that time, the idea of going far away already obsessed me. I didn't want to bear Manolito.

I started to heap handfuls of soil. I have always liked playing with soil. The topsoil was warm; that from the deeper layers held some dampness. First, I made a ford; then, a bridge. A bridge with leaves of maize and hairs of corncob on top of it, just like its surface and its sides. It was then when I heard them calling me. I stood up at once, but I crouched down again.

"Boooooy!"

The first shouts came from the side of the road; then, it seemed to me they were coming from the yard.

I went on heaping handfuls of soil. I also made a kiln, with pebbles, and I pulled up some foxgloves to put them around it. I wouldn't move from there. I promised myself to leave home forever if my father hit me again.

"Balbino!"

I was sorry for my mother and Aunt Carme, tell them to go to blazes! They had also beaten me, and they used to make me pray as well. They are all against me. From my godfather to my brother Miguel who, even the day before he set out for America, tore my hair out because I had rummaged in his toolbox.

At dusk, all of my family, and some neighbours too, were looking for me. They shouted near, far, from the farmland and from the lanes. My name came and went in the air through the village. The sun had already set and they hadn't found me yet. Many people who didn't care about me were looking for me. It was as if they were hunting a fox or chasing a wild boar. I, meanwhile, kept on making bridges and kilns, heaping stones, crushing clods.

It was getting dark when, after a soft rustle of maize leaves, I heard someone panting behind my back. I turned round. It was Pachín, the dog. Pachín was also looking for me. In fact, he had just run into me. He has his tongue hanging out and he was deadbeat. He came up to me tenderly, and we both started to frisk about. He wanted to talk to me. He, somehow, wanted to tell me that they were looking for me, and I hinted to him that I already knew it and didn't care. Pachín started to skip around me. He pulled the bridges down. I scolded him and he cringed, as if apologizing.

Night fell suddenly over the farmland. Crickets and frogs were making a row. I stretched. I put on my clogs, and, slowly, I started to go up the farmland. Pachín gave a friendly bark and went on, by my side. When I was going across the vegetable garden, I heard a distant shout calling me. I went into the house. There was nobody in. It looked like a cemetery. An empty grave.

I lay down on my bed. I dreamt of Manolito and of my father. They were playing and the landlord was having a good time. Meanwhile, I was crying. I was crying and nobody cared about me. Nobody looked at my tears, glittering on my cheeks, falling to the ground and, through the rows of maize, running away towards the river.

When I opened my eyes, I saw more than ten faces around me. I dried my tears with my shirt. Pachín stared at me from the side of my bed. I patted his neck and I fell asleep again.

9

Memoirs of a peasant boy

THE JEW

A man with the Cross led the way. The stand-ard-bearer followed him. Then went the banner, the sacred figures, the priest, old women praying, boys… How should I know!.. Like every year. The pipers were playing a march. The same old one. From time to time, a man drew up a lighter to a firework. The boys ran after its guiding stick; and when they got it, they felt like winners, as if they had found a treasure. They wanted the thread to makes kites.

The sexton was tolling the bells softly. Softly so that people paid attention to the procession; so that the praying old women could count the beads on the rosary, hear one another, and do it together like when you are reaping or thresh-ing.

I longed to go after the fireworks too, but they would never let me do it. My godfather would tell me a story about a boy who had lost his hands because he had picked up a dud shell. And my mother would hug me.

"Pray and look at the sacred figures," she would say.

I am the only one in the parish who is in steps with the adults. They want me to become a man before the right time. And I am really looking forward to growing up. However, looking forward to it is not enough. Time must go by. Meanwhile, I can't have a good time with my friends.

The sacred figures, on the portable platforms, crowded around above the people's heads. Our Lady of Carme has a neat halo, a present Mosteiro sent her from Cuba. The Jew had said, "The nabob should have given that money to the poor from the parish or bought books for the school." However, nobody trusts the Jew. Moreover, whatever he says is considered as if the devil himself had said it.

Other sacred figures were in the procession. St. Anthony, with the Baby on his lap; St. Roque, with his little dog; St. Ramón, who, as it is said, wasn't born, or came into the world when his mother had already died, or something like that. My aunt didn't know how or didn't want to tell the true story.

After going round the church, the odd group got out through the gate and walked about the streets. The pipers went on playing the same march, and the sexton, bent over the clappers, kept tolling the bells softly. Just then, something happened, I don't know what, to one of the four girls bearing St. Anthony and my mother went up to her. Meanwhile, I ran off. I fled from the procession. The man with the gunpowder set fire to a firework. When it burst, I looked up and then I started to run. I strode off, jumping like a young horse, trampling on hedges, streams, and vegetable gardens. Somehow, I finished up at the Jew's threshing floor. I no longer remembered the firework I was running after. A wire creaked and, at once, his dog, a brown and fierce dog, appeared. I moved back so that it couldn't grab me, and it was then when the sight of the owner of the house struck my eyes.

"What are you doing here," he said to me, with a hangdog look.

I didn't know what to answer. I thought of the firework, of the procession, of my mother.

"Did you intend to steal peaches?"

"No, sir, because I was told stealing is a sin."

The Jew grasped my arm and took me across the threshing floor towards the kitchen. I let myself go. The dog came behind us, licking the grease on my clogs.

Each of us sat on a stool. Everything was very clean. The kitchen was whitewashed, without soot or cobwebs, and it had a big sink, draining off into the yard.

"So, you haven't come to steal, have you?"

"It's a sin," I told him again.

"And if it wasn't a sin, would you come?"

I was thunderstruck. The Jew lighted a cigarette, rubbed his hands together, and, smiling, looked at me.

"You are Balbino, aren't you?"

"Yes, sir."

"Your parents are nice people but they are too attached to religion, they are fond of the priest and of saints. Have you been in the procession?"

"I've just come from there," I answered him.

"And what did you feel?"

I explained to him that I had heard the bells, the pipers, the old women muttering as they prayed...

"No, no," he interrupted me. "I mean if you thought of God and saints."

"I thought of the fireworks," I told him.

"Well, that's the trouble! The people who are praying pay no attention to what they are doing, either. Some ponder over the empty barns, over the taxes, over potato pest; others weave in their minds the worst pranks, and they even envy the good clothes other people might happen to wear. You are still very young and don't understand some low tricks yet. If a clog maker, for example, isn't careful with what he is doing, when the edge of the hatchet or the chisel is near his hands, he cuts them off. Well, praying is like talking to God, who is much worthy than a pair of clogs. And if God is as they say, He must already have fixed up a hell for those who mock Him that way."

I started to tremble.

"Hasn't anybody told you why they call me Jew?" he asked me.

"No, sir."

"They gave me that nickname because I'm always talking about these things. They all, in their hearts, know I'm right. But in front of the others, they offend me. I couldn't care less! I'm sorry for them, who seem to be sheep instead of men and women. Each of them has given the priest their souls to be looked after, but all the priest does is to corrupt them. Nobody thinks by himself. Thinking is a sin. Suing for justice, true justice, is a sin. And it's also a sin to have your own ideas or to search for the truth on one's own. But you are too young to understand some things. Do you attend catechism?"

"Yes, I do, sir," I told him.

"And what does the priest teach you?"

"He tells us about Trinity, about prayers, about Mass, about the four hells…"

"And do you understand all that properly?"

"…"

"They aren't all like that. The priest from Ribán explains some things from the catechism to the children. Just some things, otherwise the archbishop would already have sent him packing. But he also makes them learn Geography, History, and the customs of people from other times and other countries. He also tells them how to plant vines, when it's the best time to graft, and other things. His parishioners are fond of him. He goes to the bar with the young and, if there is a chance, he even plays a game of subastado[2] with them. And young men sing in Mass on Feast Days. He is really…"

---

[2] Subastado: A card game for three or four players in which the winner is the player who gets the points he undertakes to get. It can be played individually or in pairs.

We heard the dog bark. The Jew stood up and opened the door. I recognized my mother's voice.

My whole body ached. My father hit me with a rope. I didn't cry, but I also felt as if something that doesn't hurt ached. How could I tell! It was as if my soul ached.

Memoirs of a peasant boy

MOURNING

UNCLE Braulio died due to bad luck. It's true. However, I didn't miss him. Three years have already gone by, and they still talk about him. He was not fond of working, since he came back from military service. He was droll and kind. He was given to going on sprees and festivities. But he died. And we had to go into mourning. We all looked like priests. My everyday pair of trousers is black. Less black with every day, because its mends and patches are made of whatever is at hand. The buttons on my shirt are also black. But I don't care whether I dress in these clothes or other ones. What upsets me is to stay at home on Feast Days.

When St. Peter's or Our Lady of Carme's Day comes, I am shut in, locked in a cage like a turtledove. And all because of my uncle's death! What a misfortune! My father says that going into mourning doesn't make anybody come to life again; but my godmother starts weeping for her beloved Braulio and, again and again, she says how handsome, clever, and good he was. How should I know!.. And we keep on being in mourning.

I do remember when uncle Braulio came from Africa. He was as black as ink. He knew tales about witches and many very amusing games. He looked like a chatterbox in a fair. The young people from the village would run to our house with the idea of listening to him or playing with him. Some of them got the idea of the games and, mockingly, imitated him all around.

Lazybones as he was, my uncle knew that nowhere is bread given in return for sleeping, playing, or chatting. Therefore, he set to work. It made him very sad, but he set to. Since he was not accustomed to it, or he did not feel like being accustomed to it, he was very depressed, undertaking everything in a bad temper. That's why the affair with the cart happened. He went to Guillal Hill to fetch some dead wood and, when he was coming down, he let the animals go ahead alone, so that he could control the load with the pitchfork. The cows turned round, left the road, and the cart turned over. My uncle was trapped under the wheel. He was not even able to shout. Two men from the court were looking after him for a whole day. The doctor opened his skull to know what he had died of, or maybe he did it to steal his brain! After all, we all know too well the cart squashed him. One end of the axle had even run through his belly! However, he stubbornly said it had to be done because it was his duty, and who knows!.. He argued with my father, and my father with him, but he had it his own way. Many people went to the funeral and, even today, they talk about that misfortune in the village.

But I was not to blame for the overturning of the cart. They made me go into mourning three years ago, and I'm still in mourning, without being able to go on a spree or disguise myself as an old man during Carnival. I've never wanted to stand up to them so that I would not see my godmother weeping. She thinks the black buttons on my shirt make the purgatory my uncle surely suffers more bearable

In Lent, I felt happier than before - despite what the others did. Some people say Lent is the time to be sad because it reminds us of death, our death, and that of Our Lord. It seems to me that to think about it is good for the old. I wouldn't like to die young; but if I think twice about it, I don't care. Children are said to be angels. When Pepiño de Candau died, they put him into a white coffin, because he was an "angel", as my godmother told me. I sometimes think about the death of Our Lord. I'm shocked whenever I see him bleeding, naked, with his hands and his feet nailed to the Cross. Besides pain, it is an insult to do that to someone. Although he wasn't God, it would also be sad to look at his wounds.

I do not know why some people have a time for each thing. A time to go mad during Carnival and then to pretend they weep during Lent. But for my uncle's death, I would also have behaved like that. "Follow the crowd," my father says. But since the mourning makes me behave as if it was Lent all the time, when the true Lent comes, I see the rest of the people like me. Well, worse than me, because, even if I don't have a good time, at least I'm amused by the people, who change their faces according to the calendar.

Due to my black buttons, I spent last Carnival at home. While the others were having a good time, I had to put up with being locked in. I saw the masquerade from the dormer window.

The "couriers" led the way. They were four. Each of them was wearing a pair of gloves, white trousers, and shining jackets. They were riding spotted nags, decked out with ribbons and bright new harnesses, and covered with bells from head to tail.

They knocked at the door. My father opened it.

"Keep out," he told them.

He meant that, as we are in mourning, the masked people shouldn't start to cheer, or sing, or do anything else in front of our house. The "couriers" turned back.

However, I saw everything from the dormer window because on the other side of the road the Cordal family, who aren't in mourning for anybody and like sprees, let them in.

Before long, the generals came. They were riding merry horses - it's said they give them some wine so that they can walk haughtily - and showing off gaudy suits, three-cornered hats, boots, and spurs. On their chests, they had crosses and other junk made of tin and aluminium. Could you imagine Tomás da Eixola? He was as stiff as a poker. He had never ridden a horse before. The year before, he had disguised himself as a monk.

Eight or ten musicians from the band from Orozo came playing behind the generals. A chorus singing "A Rianxeira"[3] also turned up. A young man was carrying a handful of fireworks and, from time to time, he set one off. The boys went after it, trampling rye furrows to find the guiding stick. Meanwhile, I was locked in..!

Many people came behind, laughing at "the old". I laughed too, although I rather felt like crying because I couldn't go to the street. I laughed

---

[3] A Rianxeira: a traditional Galician song

at the music band. It wasn't music at all that they were playing! They were making such a noise as to frighten a fox. Each one howled as he liked. They had very noisy instruments: drums, small drums, trumpets, horns, and others. They were wearing old clothes, full of patches. Their faces were daubed with soot. They carried sticks tied to their bottoms with strings of wicker and laburnum.

Then I saw several things coming near: a cow and a donkey were yoked and drawing a cart with two distillers and their still on it; on another cart, there was a heap of straw, which six men, wearing "carozas de xuncas,"[4] started to thresh on the floor, each one with his flails, as they sang suitable popular songs. And behind the threshers, there came a group of blacksmiths, who put an anvil on the road and pounded it with very big hammers, as if they were hammering iron into shape. It's said that in Sarandón and in the Ulla Valley they usually cause an uproar that astonishes everyone.

One of the generals, brandishing a sword in his right hand, shouted like a madman, wishing Xacinto do Cordal a long life to share with his family.

---

[4] Carozas de xuncas: an old typical Galician hood made of rush.

"Long life," all of the riders answered at the same time.

The band played, the chorus sang, the men with the sticks started to howl, and Cordal, besides giving some money to the man with the box, took some jars of wine to the door. He invited everyone. The people laughed, sang, hailed. Everybody was having a good time. Everybody but me, who was suffering behind the dormer window.

In the morning, once the Carnival was over, they all went to church. Everybody had a long face. How funny people are! My father has told me several times that in films there are men and women you see cry, or laugh, or die and that is all a lie. They said they neither cry, nor laugh, nor die.

People must feel happy or sad for other reasons, not when the calendar tells them so. Both the masquerade spree and the sadness in Lent are things to show before the others, I think.

My godmother said the priest soiled everyone's forehead with a bit of ash while he was saying they are made of dust and, eventually, they will turn into dust again. I don't know what the point of it is. Unless it is a punishment for having enjoyed themselves during Carnival!

I wasn't to blame for my uncle Braulio being squashed by the cart. Why did they make me

25

go into this endless mourning? Sometimes I think it must be a trick to keep me at home. If that was the reason, it's worthless now. But the black buttons made me think. I think about the people who overnight sing or cry, moan or rejoice. By being always locked in, I'm compelled to look at those who walk the streets, at those who mix up tears and laughter. And I remember what Serafín, the road mender and gravedigger, used to say, "What a crazy world!"

THE GROWN-UPS

IT MUST BE a nice thing to become a grown-up. The grown-ups are the owners of themselves and of the world. They do and undo, rule, get us into wars, business, and whatever trifle happens to be. But, as my godmother says, "all that glitters is not gold". The grown-up have their own moments of sadness and uneasiness. And sometimes they do even more childish things than we do. Otherwise, they wouldn't get cross when we point out something that is wrong.

If we fight, they interfere. They don't realize our rows are nothing but games. We scratch each other and shortly after, we are friends again. They set themselves up as judges and hit anyone and anyhow, without asking anything. Our hands are small and they don't harm anybody; theirs are heavy, they hurt you. If they learnt from us, they wouldn't go to the war. In wars, they kill one another without knowing, most of the times, the reason why. It is said they pull down houses, bridges and so many things! It seems to be a game.

But a game with blood and death it is! And then, they talk about "bringing up kids…"

We come into this world with a knapsack full of questions. We take in things through our eyes, our mouths, and our ears, and we want to learn their names and meanings. But we don't always achieve it. The grown-ups get tired and tell us to be quiet or, by means of a trick, they keep us away from what we long to know. We stop talking, because it's dangerous not to be quiet at the right time. And any day, in any place, we put the question to anybody. Somebody else. Somebody else who may mislead us tells us things our parents should tell us. And our life will keep on fermenting with strange, borrowed yeast.

I think about this because I went through it, and many children go through it everywhere every day. The grown-ups forget the time when they were young. If they looked into our eyes, they would go back in time. But they don't pay attention to other problems! And they don't care about us, either!

My parents have never known how many things, even small things, make me suffer. They get on well with each other, but they sometimes quarrel, and many nights in my dreams, I'm deafened by their shouts all night long. They don't know I suffer because we are poor. I don't suffer for me - I intend to earn a lot of money when I grow up- but for them. I wish they had all sorts of things, though I may still be in rags. Brown bread disagrees with mum, but we can't afford to buy white bread. Not long ago, I saw her weeping because her wedding dress had got moth-eaten. I keep quiet, I shrink back, but those things go right into my heart. It also grieves me to have to give the landlord a smile, as if giving him half of everything we harvest was not enough.

An odd afternoon or two, while I was looking after the cattle in "La Zanca", I thought about going far away, setting off eagerly in search of money, cursing poverty. Crazy ideas that would take root in my brain! Perhaps, almost without realizing it, I had been thinking about what, after those deep thoughts, happened to me later on.

My godfather had told me the story of a wise man who ate small plants because he had nothing else, and who complained everywhere about his poverty. One day, he turned round and saw another wise man picking the small plants he had thrown away. Everything can be beaten, the best and the worst. If a man breaks his leg, another one loses both. I am poor, but Andrés do Canteiro is even poorer.

Andrés has got three brothers, all of them younger than him. His father spends the whole day in the bar and when he gets home, he is drunk. He knocks his wife and sons about. Andrés has told me that some freezing nights they had to leave home shivering because his father was going after them with a knife. They had even sometimes begged in the village.

"What about your mother? Doesn't she stand up to him?" I told him one day.

"How could she dare to stand up to him? Do you want him to kill her? She trembles like a leaf when she sees him coming."

"You have to grow up…"

Andrés laughed. As if it didn't take a long time to grow up; because time doesn't speed up or stop. It goes step by step. And we may think it goes fast or slowly depending on what we are searching.

AMERICA

MANY MONTHS ago my brother Miguel went to America. I still remember when he said goodbye to us. My mother, Aunt Carme, and my godmother were weeping. My father was as grave as a judge. Neither tears nor laughter: men are men. My godfather didn't want to go there. And Celia; we sent word to her - she is working as a servant in Loxo - but her master didn't let her come.

I was among them. Nobody paid attention to me. They hastened to give advice to the traveller while waiting for the coach to arrive. Miguel, with an "it's-all-the-same-to-me" expression on his face, agreed with everything they said. I took his hand and started to count his fingers from one side to the other, from his thumb to his little finger. I didn't say a word, but I was glad Miguel went away. Afterwards, he would tell me a lot of things. And I would tell them at school. As he paid no attention to me, I pulled him aside. He stooped and I whispered in his ear, "I want you to go away. Send me a letter from America and tell me stories about what happens there". He laughed, laid his hand on my head, and ruffled my hair. I felt as if I had an itchy body.

We heard the horn of the "Modelo". It came as fast as it could, with a lot of boxes and baskets on top of it. My mother and godmother were kissing and hugging Miguel, and they kept on weeping. My father raised the suitcase up to where the conductor was. It was a brand new suitcase, made by the carpenter from Quintela. Then, he hugged my brother for a moment. Before getting on the coach, Miguel laid his hand around my neck, gave me a kiss on my cheek and, saying, "bye, Balbino", he went away as quick as lightning. I was bewildered. I could say or do nothing. The "Modelo" set off slowly. Miguel looked at us as he waved his handkerchief.

"Don't give up going to Mass," my mother shouted.

"God bless you! Don't go downhill!" said my mother as she dried her tears.

And aunt Carme gave him her last advice, which I didn't understand properly.

"Watch out for women!"

"Stop shouting," my father told them, as he took me by the hand. "Do you think he can hear you? Can't you see how far off the coach is?"

The "Modelo" was running fast. It looked like a cloud flying at ground level, through pinewoods, through vineyards. Miguel was on it.

Time went by and we didn't get a letter. My mother prayed night and day, and she lit a candle to Our Lady of Carme so that the ship my brother was voyaging in didn't sink. At last, one day we got a letter. Miguel was fine. He was working at Uncle Xaquin´s shop. He wore fine clothes and shoes each day. Besides, he was off on Saturday afternoons; he travelled by bus and ate white bread, cheese, and other kind of food every day. That was a living!

"When I grow up, I'll go to America," I said.

And my father interrupted me.

"When you grow up, you'll learn a trade and you'll be here for the rest of your life, without wandering all over the world.

"What about Miguel?"

"Miguel is already far away. And, that's enough".

I thought about white bread, about cheese, and about fine clothes. They say you spend nine days without seeing land. Only water, night and day.

My godfather, who is not very talkative, was sitting by the fireplace; he turned round and said,

"Listen, boy. I want you to get what I'm going to tell you into your head. I learnt it when I was as young as you are now."

"To America men go,
To America to earn.
And America is here
For those who want to work."

I keep quiet. I'm already fed up with their telling me I'm too young to understand certain things. Perhaps going or not going to America was only an old people's tale. You have to grow up. No longer did I pay attention to their talk. I started to slice, with a knife, the root of a turnip I had found under the trough. My father and godfather kept on talking.

"I talk to the boy like that, but I'm sure America is something different," said my father. "There are other chances. You can become rich if you are clever and you know how to save money. But for the objections they raise, I would…"

"You don't know what you are talking about," my godfather interrupted him. "There are no more advantages in America than here. Nobody else but me, who spent too many years there, can tell you that. America is a trap. Those who fall into it don't warn those who arrive later. First of all, you lose customs, ways of living from your own country. Then, you lose happiness. Finally, most of the times, you lose everything. It's like when a tree is pulled up and its roots remain naked, without any soil"

My father talked about those who come back with a lot of money and uphold their new country by buying houses and everything they find. And my godfather told him that there were more men who couldn't come back, and if you were to die poor, it would be better to close your eyes where you were born. He said that some of them make you laugh, or disgust you, when they turn up with a new way of speaking, with a gold chain around their bellies, and a car, which they try to drive along our lanes. What a sarcastic man my godfather is! When dad told him something about those who were harder workers, he angrily rose to his feet.

"Everybody works more than enough there," he said. "There may be some slothful people, but one swallow does not make a summer. Lazy people don't go there. They know food is provided freely nowhere, and, for some reason or other, they prefer to be idle in the village.

What the work emigrants do in excess helps the other to grow. But it depraves them. They think they were thrown into this world to pull a yoke night and day. "You must not carry anything to extremes," they say. Here, they give up everything they were doing to go on a spree as soon as they hear drums play in a chestnut grove; and there, they work all the time without knowing, most of the time, when it's Sunday. I went through it. With the same effort, they would live better in their own country. And they would live in what is theirs, without being spoiled."

They kept quiet for a while. I went on thinking about white bread and cheese and about Miguel's good luck. My father didn't feel easy in his mind, giving up all that without clarifying it, and he said that young people longed to go abroad and learn things; and then, my godfather made another speech, saying that the worst thing was that young people were the ones who went away. He also wished it was just an old people's folly because the old are a dead loss. But the people who work are those who go away, and the country is full of old people and children.

He also said that going away to learn things was a cock-and-bull story, because most of those who emigrate leave the country when they have enough sense to understand and reason out things, and then they become puppets. He said they changed their language, exchanging it for a babble they can't even understand themselves. My godfather compared it with a blackbird in a cage. It's said that we can feed it as we like and make it whistle a popular tune, but it doesn't get used to it. One day, it flies to the moor and on the moor, it's a stranger, a spoiled blackbird. That was a good story, wasn't it?

My father said if people didn't go away, there wouldn't be enough space here for all of us.

"There is enough space for everybody," my godfather answered. "The country is still here to be exploited. If, overnight, they didn't let people leave the country, we could have a revolution, which is the thing to do, and we could live the way we deserve, without suffering hard work abroad."

They kept on arguing, each one giving his reasons. I went to the threshing floor. I didn't enjoy that conversation. I understood a few things. Most of them, I did not. Grown-ups' talk! My godfather shouted, loud enough to make you deaf, and my father could hardly butt in. And everything happened because I'd said I'd go to America when I grew up. Could you believe it? It reminds me of the fire. A small match can burn a straw loft or a granary.

I made the face of a doll out of the root of the turnip. In each eye socket I set a kidney bean. I laid it in hole in the wall, as it was a sacred figure.

Miguel also used to make dolls, and carts and ploughs out of pine barks. Is he likely to make them in America? Uncle Xaquín might not

37

let him do them. And he may not let him write a letter either. He has only sent one letter. When is he going to write to me? I want him to tell me about whatever happens there. We agreed that when he went away. He may have forgotten it.

PACHIN

THERE WAS A TIME, they say, when animals could speak. Tales! I don't mind if you tell them to babies still at the breast, but don't tell them to me, who has already gone through many things. Truth is being remade every day. I have heard nothing serious about "The Guardian Angel" or "The Magi" for a long time. And who knows how many of the things I consider to be true today will change inside of me. I'm moving away from the cradle, so to speak.

It would be funny if animals could speak like us. Birds, the cattle, hares. What a row! They may understand one another without talking, or they may not need to understand one another. There are a lot of men and women who speak the same language, and yet they don't understand one another.

My mother has told me several times she would like to see, at least for a minute, the river empty. So would I. However, I would be even more pleased to hear a conversation between cows, pigs, or chickens. How many things you think about! And everything happened since I had Pachín.

Pachín did speak. In his way, he did it. He spoke with his eyes, with his tail, with his legs. I understood him as if he uttered words. He didn't look like a dog. His understanding was as good as that of a human being.

Before I was born, they had had Rabeno. Someone had given it to my godfather in Silleda. They said it was big, fierce, wolf crossbreed. Miguel had known it. However, one day Rabeno fell ill and they had to kill him. My father shot him dead with a shotgun, behind the straw loft.

Pachín was quite small, brown-haired. He had a freckle on his muzzle, which looked nice on it when he was shredding his food. He liked to make a row every morning. As a greeting. His jolly barks were addressed to trees and birds. What a good time he had jumping up and down over the threshing floor!

Dogs are said to howl when they smell out death. Pachín never howled. Either he had a bad sense of smell or he didn't like announcing burials. He was glad, friendly. He lacked nothing but laughing. He might laugh, I guess, because sometimes he showed his teeth like when one is happy.

He was the funniest dog in the area. Everybody liked him. The clog maker from Ribán had given him to my father, in return for him having whetted a scythe. I brought him in my lap.

"It's going to be fierce," somebody said, "because its hard palate is black."

He, however, wasn't right. Pachín might have realized that the wrong thing to do was biting people's ankles. He would get angry if he was urged to attack, but he didn't like to seize anybody in his mouth.

When they left me alone at home, I used to play with him. Together we would run all over the vegetable garden as if we were chasing rabbits. Then, we would sit down by the big cherry tree. My sweat slipped down my cheeks and Pachín panted quickly, his tongue hanging out.

He was the envy of some boys. They were annoyed about me having such a dog. Pachín realized it and decided not to put up with anybody's games. When a naughty boy threw stones at him, or urged him to attack, he jumped on him in a flash, growling, showing his teeth.

"Don't get mad, Pachín," I would say to him. "You don't bite them, but you chase them away; you make them uneasy, and one day they are going to break your back."

Pachín would lay his front legs on my chest; he would look at me with his big eyes and would wag his tail. It was as if, in a rushed way, he was saying, "leave me alone, I know what I'm doing."

Aunt Carme goes to the well with a bucket every morning. Besides water, she usually brings some news. One day, she told she had seen the blacksmith's wife crying because the night before the fox had got into the henhouse and taken nine hens away. First, it had moved about the tiles on the roof, and then, finding out that the crossbeams were thick, it had cunningly dug a tunnel under the door.

That morning I had gone with the cattle to "A Zanca Vella", and while I was looking for nests, I found the fox's den in a furze-covered place. The nine hens were there, dead. Blood and feathers were all around.

I left the cattle there and hastened away to the blacksmith's to tell him about what I'd found. Pachín was running by my side. A neighbour, who is a hunter, said that we should do everything very carefully, otherwise the fox would realize we had found its den, and there would be no way of taking revenge.

They went to the chemist, who asked them to take, at least, two hens to him. And so they did. He cut their necks and put some poison inside them. They laid them in the den again to poison the fox. But it didn't happen that way. The one that appeared dead after two days in "A Zanca Vella" was Pachín, my friend Pachín.

When I saw him dead, lying down among some heather, I couldn't believe my eyes. As I have so many dreams, for a moment I thought I was dreaming; it couldn't be true. But I was not dreaming. Pachín had died. He had fallen in the trap set for the fox.

I took him back from the moor. With a small hoe, I dug a deep, long hole in the vegetable garden, and I buried his body. I think I cried. I'm not ashamed of saying I cried. I tenderly covered him with damp soil; as if I was wrapping him up with a blanket.

As a gravestone, I planted a cherry tree over my friend. When it sprouted, I thought I could see one of Pachín´s eyes or teeth in every bud. And I fancied tender barks were coming from the roots.

Memoirs of a peasant boy

REMAINS

IT WAS OVER. Our Lady of Carme´s Day was over, and I hadn't been allowed to go to the chestnut grove. I'm already used to staying at home, as if it was a prison. What really makes me suffer is that nobody cares about me. Being in mourning for uncle Braulio is like a rope squeezing my neck.

In the morning, I went to Mass with my godmother. I had grumbled, but she had taken a club and started to hit me. I had not been able run away. My godmother is always telling me about Hell, where, it's said, there are kilns burning forever and wheels with knives always chopping the souls of the mean people who go there. She gets angry when I answer her back by laughing at those frightening stories. She gets furious. Every Sunday the same thing happens. Our parents and our godparents seem to have been born to make us go to the places we don't want to go. I never feel like going to Mass or saying the rosary at night. But I must do it by hook or by crook.

Therefore, we went to Mass early in the morning. The high solemn Mass was at eleven, but you are not allowed to attend it when you are in mourning. In the afternoon, I played billarda[5] alone on the threshing floor, and when night fell, I went up to the loft so that, from its small window, I could have a look at the chestnut grove where the open-air dance was taking place.

I stayed there for a good while. A gentle and refreshing breeze was blowing on my forehead. A lot of crickets and toads were making a racket in the vegetable garden. The chestnut grove was lit by very nice fair-lights… The bands from Arca and Ribeira were playing and the people were dancing. Cheers, popular songs, shouts from the children, the smell of octopus. All this came up to me. The fairy-lights swung in the air. Among the people and oaks, there rose a cloud of dust, which spread outwards.

I had already heard many of the songs the bands played. The echo resounded far away, even in the most distant part of the oak wood. It looked as if a bunch of ghosts were carrying

---

[5] Billarda: a Galician game played with two sticks, one shorter than the other. The player, using the longer one as a bat, must strike the sorter one in order to throw it away as far as possible.

away the racket on their backs. I, sometimes, felt as if I was flying, as if the music took me away from the loft and carried me through the air. Many stars were shining up in the sky. As if they were glancing at the uproar from the grove. I stared at one that was twinkling brighter than the others. I fancied it was pulling me up. I felt I was tied to it, as if in an embrace. I gave her a kiss, and shortly after, we started to dance, to the sound of the music...

I was falling asleep. I had got up early to go to the moor with my father, and I was sleepy. The idea of having danced with the star made me laugh. I glanced at the chestnut grove. The people were still having a good time. The fairy-lights were shining brightly. I closed the small window and went to bed. I could hear the music from my bed. I thought of the remains. As I hadn't gone to the open-air dance, I would search for the remains. After St. Roque's Day, I had found five pesetas and a handkerchief.

I dreamt of uncle Braulio. He hadn't died; he had gone to Africa again. The mourning was a trick my godmother and my parents had made up, just to keep me locked in. Tales that hit your brain when you are sleeping!

I got up very early. Quietly and quickly, I fled to the chestnut grove. Other boys also used to search for the remains, but no one had come yet.

The ground was uneven. It was always like that after an open-air dance. There were some corks and pieces of paper among the oak trees. The grass and some brushwood were squashed. The carts where octopus and wine were sold had left their tacks. It smelt of green. Smell of fennel, calamintha, scrub covered with dew. The sun had started to rise behind the mountain and it was spreading its beams. I looked around and saw nobody. I thought about how things change overnight. The day before it looked like a swarm. Now I was alone. As if they all had died or they had been nothing but a parade of ghosts. As if I had nothing to do with the nature of those people. What a funny thought! The sun and I were rummaging in the chestnut grove. Had the sun also come in search of the remains? At least, it had come to light it up for me.

I went around the bandstand several times; I walked along the road for a while, I went all over the field, and I found nothing at all. Just when I was coming back home along the path, my eyes found something shining by a heather brush. I got closer and picked it up. It was a neat wooden box. Its lock was made of white metal.

My heart was beating hard. I had to stop my legs from starting to run and tell them all about my good luck. I had never had in my hands such a beautiful thing. At once, I thought it over. As soon as I got home with that treasure, everyone, to start with my godmother, would make me look for its owner and give it to him. I couldn't steal, but you don't steal what you find. After all, it was neither a sickle, nor a hoe, nor a lot of money. Yet, I felt uneasy. I didn't care about the owner of the box! I had to hide the happiness I felt, and that made me suffer.

I started going down the moor. I crossed the road; I went on over the farmland until I got to the bank of the river. The people who had gone on a spree the day before woke up late. I didn't let them see me.

The sun was already burning. Everything was quiet. You could only hear the persistent din of the water swirling around a rock, and the warbling of the early birds.

I stood gaping, looking at the box. What a nice toy! It was long, shiny, made of wood with yellow grains. I shook it. It was shut. Something that moved inside aroused my curiosity. I longed to open it, but I wasn't able to do it, at least without breaking its lock.

That had really been a lucky search. But, what could I do with the box? I first thought about taking it home and hiding it in the straw loft or in the shed, among the logs. But, sooner or later, they would find it. That's why I hid it in the yard. I pulled up a bush and, near its root,

I buried, surrounded by ferns, my treasure in the sand.

"Where have you been?" My mother asked.

"I've been searching for the remains," I told her.

"You certainly have! And what did you find? The sky above you?"

"I didn't find anything at all, but as you didn't let me go there yesterday, at least…"

"Do not forget we are in mourning."

"…I wanted to see the chestnut grove after the open-air dance."

I thought they would tell me off even more than they did. I'm already used to it. But my father didn't say a word, neither did my godmother.

I spent the whole day thinking of the box. And at night I dreamt of it. I dreamt I'd opened it with the help of a locksmith. Inside of it, there were gold coins and small precious stones, like those in the money box of the Count of Monte Cristo - a very rich character who is said to be in one of the Jew's books. I also dreamt I'd gone to Santiago to buy an aeroplane. A real aeroplane! I learnt how to fly it and started travelling around the world, over the clouds. I flew to Labacolla, Madrid, France, and many other places. Flying was smooth, and the plane ran like the wind. Sometimes I fancied I was going to crash against a rock or to smash into a field, but nothing happened. However, just when I was at the best bit, when I was arriving in America to see my brother Miguel, I woke up. My father was by my bed.

"I heard you nattering and I came here," he said to me, laughing. "You were saying something about a "box", an "aeroplane", "gold". What were you dreaming of?"

"I don't know. Trifles. I can dream in spite of the mourning, can't I?"

My father laughed again. He tucked me up and went away. In the morning, I took the cattle to graze on the moor. I thought about the small box over and over again. I couldn't get it out of my mind. I felt like taking it in my hands and caressing it. And after dreaming, I yearned to open it. I almost swore I would even hit it with a stone to know what there was inside of it.

That morning seemed to me longer than any other. Time did not go by. I wasn't amused by listening to birds or blowing the whistle. My senses were in the yard. I saw the bush where I had buried the treasure in every clump of furze, heather, or broom.

At last, the sun was high. I came back home, and I concealed my uneasiness as much as I could. As soon as I arrived, I took a hoe and told them I was going to divert water from the stream into the field.

I ran to the yard. I laid down the hoe and got ready to visit the hiding place. It didn't take me a long time to reach the bush. I dug in the sand until I found the box. There it was, as nice and shiny as the day before. My heart was beating hard. There it was with its yellow grains, the metal lock, and that inner noise that made me be uneasy. I remembered the gold coins and the aeroplane. What things one may dream of! Even so, I didn't dare to break the lock, though I longed to do it. My eyes didn't get tired of look-ing at it, neither my hands of caressing it. I even reached the point of loving it more than all of my family. To me it was like a star. Something you love a lot, but there's no way of telling it so. I've never been a lucky boy. Not when I play bil-larda or when I get into a scrap at school. And suddenly, my lovely box! I was the luckiest boy. All at once, I was fantastically lucky.

I stood up and looked around. I was alone on that side of the yard.

Everything looked nice to me. As if I was in Heaven, or something like that. Smell of ferns, water rippling, butterflies coming and going.

But I had to go. It was late, and I didn't want anyone to see me there. I gave the box a kiss and buried it in the sand again, with the idea of coming back to be by its side again in the afternoon. I took the hoe and headed for the field.

The sun was burning my head and the back of my neck. I diverted the water and led it along the water-channel, removing stubble and dead leaves. My father didn't let me work in the vineyard or plough, but he had got me used to me looking after the meadow. While the water was flowing, I sat down in the shade of a birch tree. I was dripping sweat. There was thunder in the air. Dark clouds were hiding the sun. With the hoe on one shoulder, I set out. I still hadn't reached home when I heard drops like coconuts falling.

It was raining cats and dogs. The roads were getting flooded. Stones and brushwood were rolling down El Castro. Lightning and thunder shook the Earth. It was raining the whole afternoon. And all night long.

In the morning it was still raining. From my bedroom, I saw the river outside its bed. Outside in the yard, my poor, rattling treasure! It was scattered somewhere in the nearby farmland. The flood had swept it away!

When it stopped raining and the river began to lower, I went up to it.

I longed to bring it to book for its prank. It had carried off my box. It had taken my happiness away; the illusion of being, at last, a lucky boy because I had found something in the remains in the chestnut grove.

The gold coins and the aeroplane went away. I dreamt night and day, for nothing.

The bush was ruined, its leaves withered, turned upside down, covered with mud. I laid my hands on my face and started to weep.

ELADIA

ONE DAY I went to the fair with Aunt Carme. I have always enjoyed going to the fair, even when I had to lead a pig with a rope or carry a basket full of peaches they would put on my head. When night fell, I was tired but happy, because we used to have octopus for lunch and, just before coming back home, used to buy some nicknacks.

This time, my aunt had taken me there so that I could bring a bundle of cabbage home. How I wished I hadn't gone there! As I was crossing Pottery Square, I saw Eladia. She was buying some earthenware bowls. Eladia! Could my family just imagine…! On that early occasion, I already felt like running away, leaving home one night, and coming back as a young man: when I could speak to each and everyone. As time went by, that idea faded from my mind until, like when you reopen an old wound, I stared at Eladia once again. I was about to shout. I scrambled out through the carts, so she couldn't see me.

Some neighbours had asked me why I had left school.

"What a great reader you were!"

"What a good memory you had!"

"I've already learnt everything. There's nothing in it for me any longer," I would tell them jokingly so they would shut up.

There are things I don't understand. Perhaps I'll have to grow up to understand them. Things my body gradually discloses; things I feel as time goes by. I don't know why but I am ashamed to talk about them at home.

I remember the day when I went to school for the first time. My aunt led me by the hand. Don Alfonso, the schoolteacher, wrote down my name in a piece of paper, asked me a few questions, and made me sit down on a bench by other boys.

I already knew some things. I already knew the catechism and I could add up. Don Alfonso liked those advantages. It didn't take me a long time to get ahead of my class-mates.

The school is in Mrs. Isaura´s Hall. You go in through a main door, which is rotten. There is a circular patch of honeysuckle and two very big walnut trees. The flight of steps leading to the veranda is made of stone. The joins between the steps are mouldy because of the rain. The school is big, but it's empty most of the time. Few boys go there. Sometimes nobody goes there.

"They only need to be able to write their names, that's enough for them, who will till land," people say.

Don Alfonso was a mean person. He explained too little and smacked too much. What a way to smack and tug our ears! My godmother says, "Spare the rod and spoil the child"; in other words, she believes the proper thing to soothe us is to give us a beating.

Many boys missed class; they didn't go to school because they were afraid. And because they didn't understand Don Alfonso's way of speaking. He's said to have come from Andalusia. I also found it difficult to understand him. He spoke quickly and pronounced badly. To make matters worse, he had a hoarse voice. He didn't understand our language either. That's why, filled with anger, he rose to his feet and shouted like one possessed.

The Jew, who always says whatever he wants, accosted Don Alfonso one day and called him all the names under the sun.

"Do you think boys are calves? Do you think beating them is the right thing? Sir, you must realize all these annoyances will soon come to an end. All of a sudden, matters will take their course. If you don't understand our language, go back to your own country. We will not change our language. One more thing: stop teaching them about kings and battles that are useless. Moreover, give up schooling them in prayers and religious instructions. Let them learn catechism at home, if their parents want to. School has its own aim. That's the way it is."

After the ticking-off, the Jew talked to some neighbours, and though they weren't fond of him, they agreed he was right. Together they signed a sheet of paper, I don't know where they sent to, asking to take Don Alfonso away from the village. In fact, he went away in a month's time. Shortly after, Eladia came.

Eladia is very young. She is twenty, I guess. I'm surprised she is a schoolteacher, as young as she is. She was born in Betanzos. She speaks Galician to us. I got fond of her at once. How loving! How cheerful!

The day she arrived many of the neighbours went to the school. Everybody told her they were eager to help her in whatever she needed.

"Thank you very much. Now, I want you to send your children to school," she replied in her tender voice.

Then, she asked us several things. I wanted her to notice me. And she did notice me, because I answered some History questions better than anybody else did.

"Balbino," she said, "you seem better than the others. Don't show off, since we all ignore more than we know. If some day I'm ill or I have to travel, you will be in my place."

I was delighted. Filled with envy, the other boys looked at me.

At home, they were amazed at my efforts to go to school every day. Many times I have got up at three in the morning to crush or to tie sheaves. I would wash my face in the brook, and at eight I was in the Hall: my arms tired, cuts on my hands, and an itch on my neck.

Eladia looked like an angel to me; a creature fallen from Heaven, without strength to do anybody harm. An impossible dream! I didn't get tired of staring at her hair, as curly as the nest of a sparrow, at her careful, lovely hands, at her sweet face, at her eyes, at her figure... How should I know!... I wished I could always be with her, always by her side. One day she gave me a kiss because I'd been able to explain the discovery of America, and I felt a kind of bubbling in my chest. I had never felt anything like that before. My heart was beating hard, and my blood seemed to have flooded my whole body.

In the parish, everybody said I was a witty boy. They also said I should study at Santiago University. People like talking just for talking´s sake. If you want to study in Santiago, you need money; and my parents are poor. I learnt a lot of things, that's true, but their only worth was to be appreciated by Eladia.

Eladia lived in a new house near the church. Her sister lived with her. The poor girl wasn't beautiful, and you could only see her at Sunday Mass, or when she was watering the front garden. I would pass by there whistling when night had fallen, heading nowhere, and I would check cunningly if the schoolteacher's eyes were watching from behind the windowpanes. No chance! How far away from my eagerness she was! After all, I was only a boy.

One day Eladia didn't turn up at school. The other boys went back home, but I went to her house. I ran like hell. I imagined a lot of things. Had she left the parish without notice? Had she died? I've never prayed, not even when my godmother compels me, but in this awkward situation, I prayed and even offered money to the Souls in Purgatory. When I got there, I was puffing. Her sister opened the gate and told me it was only flu what she had. She let me in. Eladia was in bed. What a nice bedroom! Pictures, jars, flowers! Surrounded by silken clothes and white-washed walls, I was ashamed of my clogs and mends. I stood still, without breathing a word. She smiled.

"Get closer, Balbino," she told me.

We were speaking for a good while. We talked about school, about hardships in the country, about the utterly wretched lives of peasants. She told me how people from the seashore live and work. Her father was a fisherman, and he got drowned. Two teardrops rolled down her cheek. I felt like wiping them with my handkerchief, but I did not dare. Neither could I tell her everything I wanted. My heart started to beat hard and I got tongue-tied. How fainthearted I am!

At home, they all were happy because I, such a young boy, was going to take the teacher's place at school.

It was hard to impose my authority on my classmates, who called me "the wise man" and other things, but I got it. I had been in charge of school for three days. In the parish, nobody had ever seen such a thing, and everyone respected me. Could they only imagine my uneasiness! I only studied so that Eladia would be fond of me. On the third day, I felt more confident, tougher. And my despair drove me to poke about in the drawers of Eladia´s table. The first thing I found was a handkerchief. It had the same scent as her bedroom. I held on to it. I also took a little portrait of her, in which she was laughing, holding tightly a bunch of carnations against her body.

I slept that night with Eladia´s handkerchief under my face. What a pleasant scent! I gave her portrait a thousand and one kisses. It was as if she was there, smiling, staring at me. I dreamt I already was a man and we were going to get married. I was also a schoolteacher. Each of us worked in a school. Eladia hugged me, tickled me, and we even slept together. What things you dream of! Sometimes it would be better not to wake up...

Every night I would go to her house to tell her what had happened at school. I wished she were like that for a long time, since those visits, chatting with her as an equal, were for me a privilege. How many times I was about to tell her what I felt! But I did not dare.

My legs trembled, I felt my forehead getting cold..., and I kept quiet. I was afraid she might laugh at me, or she might get angry and tell the story to my mother. They would all know it, and I'd have to run away from the village.

On Sunday - she was already fine - I saw her walking hand-in-hand with a young man along the riverside. I felt very sad. I felt like bumping into them and insulting them. But I didn't do it. I waited until night fell. They were sitting in the garden. Walking cautiously by the wall, I moved towards them. They didn't see me. They were speaking softly and I didn't understand a word. In the moonlight I saw them sitting side by side and kissing each other. I turned back home angrily, weeping. I was tempted into tearing up Eladia´s portrait and dumping her handkerchief, but I caressed them more lovingly than ever before.

The day after, I couldn't get up, I had fever, and my legs and head were aching. My godmother provided me with a lot of remedies.

"I have already told you something wrong was happening to the boy," she shouted to my father. "I have seen him sickly, weakened, lost in his thoughts for a long time. You insist that is only because he gets up early, works hard and goes to school daily. I don't know what it is, but I don't like it"

For several days, I was swallowing the mixtures my godmother wanted. Eladia came to see me, escorted by that man I loathed. I hid my head and refused to pay attention to them. My mother offered them liqueur and, as a compliment, she told them of our lives. I lost patience and felt shame.

One day, on seeing I didn't get better, they called for the doctor from San Mamede. He examined my eyes, my throat, searched my whole body, and told them to give me some medicines my father went and bought in Santiago. Soon after this, I got up and started to walk outside the house. I hadn't seen Eladia since that day, and I longed to see her. I wanted to tell her the reason of my ache and at the same time beg her pardon for not having paid attention to her when she had come to see me. But I knew the truth at once. I knocked at her door, but neither she nor her sister appeared. Fortunately, a neighbour told me the whole story. Eladia had left the parish to come back no more. She had married far away, to the man who used to come and see her.

I felt as if a rock had fallen upon me; I felt like dying or running away. It was as if I had an empty heart. How should I know!.. No matter how many times I think about some things, I don't manage to understand them. I always thought I had seen Eladia when I bumped into a girl who looked like her. One night I dreamt there was a fair, or an open-air dance, where all the women were Eladia. And from then on, I've liked other young women, though not as much as her. As if I was a young man!

I swore to go to school no longer. And I did not go.

Between the sheets of a book, I laid her handkerchief and portrait.

But I had never imagined seeing Eladia at the fair. Time had faded away my memories. And now they all woke up suddenly. Because time both treats injuries and make trees rot.

St. JOHN´S NIGHT BONFIRE

THIS YEAR they let me go there. And I felt as relieved as if I had grown up all of a sudden. It wasn't as good as all that, but since I had been shut in…

Secundino, Lelo, and Moncho were going with me. Then Serafin do Pesco joined us. We were taking ropes and sickles with us. From the tool shed I'd chosen the newest sickle, one that had just been whetted.

We went over moors and pastures; we walked across fields and meadows, and along the river-side. Each of us brought his bundle. The scent of grass and the excitement of the bonfire pushed us. No longer were there tired legs or hurting clogs.

It was getting dark. At the crossroads, we laid down our bundles and sat down on them. Some young women walked past to the well.

"Make a large fire," they, laughing, told us.

A creaking, cow-drawn cart filled with sheaves came forward, behind it, a man and a woman.

"So, we are going to have a bonfire, are we?" The man hit my bundle with his stick.

"Yes, sir," I said.

"Boys don't forget St. John's Night", her wife added. Then, they followed the cart along the road to the village.

That afternoon - the first afternoon they let me go there - I learnt the names of the sacred plants for ever: snapdragons, mugworts, green pine needles, leaves of chestnut tree and birch tree, branches of olive tree, laburnums, bay leaves, daphnes, branches of walnut tree, swede flowers, and rosemary.

We piled them up in the middle of the cross-roads, and after having dinner, we set fire to them. More people were coming. Young people, old people, boys… Everybody. Jars of wines, tambourines, and a bagpipe! Uncle Anselmo da Regueira told us that in his day bonfires were brighter. Nonsense! Old people are always saying the same about things young people do.

The dark smoke, thick and big rings of smoke, rose straight up in the still air, slowly, tiredly. The night was quiet, calm as if the world was about to come to its end. We, however, kept on poking the fire while young men and young women, hand-in-hand, were jumping over the bonfire saying,

"Save me
St. John's fire
Don't let snakes or dogs bite me"

The piper began to play. Men and women were dancing around the fire. They looked crazy. From time to time they drank wine and cheered loudly.

It was after midnight. After such a long toil, I was tired. I sat down by the side of the road, next to the sickle and the rope. People went on dancing wildly. It was a never-ending muiñeira[6]. The reed and the bag didn't want to get rid of the piper and dragged him along over stubble and stones. And they were all drinking and cheering loudly! The smoke didn't rise any longer and spread out and mixed with the men and women. Shortly after, nothing was left but smoke and ashes. Nobody remained but the piper, bleeding, writhing around the crossroads. But it didn't take him a long time to disappear in the smog. The bagpipe became quiet, but it started to swell, to get frightening bigger and bigger. The wind blew it, but it didn't make it play. Till, with a deafening noise, it burst.

---

[6] Muiñeira: typical Galician dance.

67

I woke up.

Many people had already gone away. To put an end to St. John's Night bonfire, they launched a firework, which, actually, made me wake up. My father took me by the hand and we went away. Along the road we met some young men carrying half-burnt laburnums. It's said they throw them onto roofs to keep witches away.

The night was warm and a bit mysterious. Frogs were croaking in the vegetable gardens. Every little sound made me tremble. My father, moreover, began to tell me some things people used to do that night. He told me there are young women who leave whites of eggs on windowsills, and in the morning, they try to guess their future from the shape the egg has. Other young women, with broken hearts, take small bits of laburnum and wrap them in pieces of paper, on which they write their lover's names, and they lay their little dowries on their beds, under the pillow. On St. John's Day, early in the morning, they open the wrappings, and if a flower has sprouted, it means the man whose name is on the paper will come back again.

My father was chatty. He told me about young women who, early in the morning on St. John's Day, wash their faces with water in which the day before they put different kinds of herbs; he also told me that there are places where people keep the cattle and sick people's clothes out, and that witches appear

How can I remember all the things he told me! Both the dream I had dreamt at the cross-roads and those stories made my hair stood on end. Luckily, we get home very soon.

"Tomorrow we have to get up early, boy," my father said.

"As usual..."

"Not as usual," he interrupted me kindly. "We have to see the sun dance."

We did see it dancing. We were at Agra Vella. The sky was as clean as it can be. We had gone there to harrow so that we could sow with early corn. Slowly, behind the hill, it began to rise and spread its shining beard over the land. Then, we made the cattle stop and looked at the horizon.

Since it was daylight, I wasn't afraid, but the sun, as my father had told me beforehand, was dancing, at dawn, like a madman.

Memoirs of a peasant boy

DEATH

ONE MORNING I was woken up by the anguished cries of my godmother and my mummy. Heartbreaking cries as if they were on fire. Their echoes climbed up the walls. They went and came ripping through the air. I felt as if my soul was being torn to pieces.

My godfather had just died.

The doctor had already told us that, due to his heart problem, he would pass away unexpectedly, without a word, without suffering. And it must have happened like that because I had never heard him groan. The day before, he had even been crooning in the kitchen.

I got up out of bed as quick as lightning, but instead of going out, I went to the window, rested my elbows on its sill and, foolishly, I stared at the river. I don't know what the river has to do with my godfather's death, but the truth is that there I stood, watching the river flowing. Maybe, without thinking, I was comparing it with people's life. I had read something about it at school. I had read that rivers flow into the sea and, in the same way, in the same hurry, we stride along towards death. If you think it twice, you feel like crying.

The sun rose sluggishly over O Castro. First, it peeped with its burning eye, and then it spread its warm beams over the world. I had never noticed such a clever trick.

Before the sun came, hoarfrost was on everything: on the road, on the moor, on the farmland. It melted slowly. After that, a layer of sticky mud was the only thing that remained.

A creaking cart went by. The bulls led the way, and after them, with one hand on the cart and the other holding a stick, there walked a tired man in rags. It was time to plough. The cart was loaded with dung up to the top of the cart ladders. It gave out smoke. At the back of it there was a sort of a little wall made of planks. I liked the smell of dung, and I also liked throwing it onto the cart with a fork. When the amount of dung was too heavy, I would lift it with my hands or my father would come and help me.

Shouting, my godmother went on grieving. It was sad hearing her. If it was in the night-time, I would be afraid. She spoke to my godfather in a rushed way, though he, being dead… I did not want to listen to it, I did want to be far away, but I couldn't, unless I threw myself on the road. At least, they didn't remember me. Nobody called me. And I was still standing there, resting my elbows on the sill.

The frost had already melted. Women and men, carrying hoes and rakes on their shoulders, went by. It was not only the right time to sow wheat, so that ergot couldn't grow on it, but also a nice day to work. The sun was shining and the soil was dry. Everybody was moving about. Some people loosened clods with hoes. Others spread dung with forks. Then, they started to sow. Immediately afterwards, they cut furrows with a plough. The mouldboard pushed furrow slices to one side, and the people who followed it hid the uncovered dung with hoes and rakes. Boys led the animals and frightened off the wagtails that were eating seeds.

I liked gazing at furrows, especially at those done by handy people. They looked like a drawing, with loops and turns done according to the length and width of each field.

Once again, I looked at the river and compared it with life; with our own life; with the lives of those who were ploughing, of those who were far away, or went on board, or were still to be born. What an incredible parade the world is! What a fair, where incessantly some people arrive and others depart!

I heard the door creak. It was my mother. She was coming up to me rubbing her eyes with the apron. Weeping, she took me in her arms.

"What a misfortune, my dear! Your godfather has died."

I didn't know what to say. I was really sorry because my godfather did love me. And I loved him! He used to advise me, to tell me stories, and he had never once tried to hit me. Sometimes he was in no mood for jokes and I moved away from him, but once it was over, he was chatty, glad.

I went downstairs. The door of the house was wide open; the kitchen full of people. Everybody was arranging something. One person had told the news to the doctor and our relatives, another one had gone to the court. Somebody had taken the cattle to graze; someone had gone to toll the bells. Everything was like that. As they came in, they would lay their hands on one of our shoulders and say, sorrowfully, that my godfather's death was also a great grief to them.

The bells had already tolled in mourning. That's something I've also thought about. A bell not only peals joyfully on the eve of feast-days, but also gives notice of a death. It both warns of fire and calls people to thresh. It always has the same sound, but we understand its speech, its language, which sometimes is happy and sometimes not so much.

What a noise! It's nice to see how all the neighbours help. Death is like a heartfelt bond.

When we confront it, we pretend to be brothers. And those who didn't talk to one other start to talk and help one another when there is a dead person. But I don't get used to it. Outsiders arrange everything and they don't even ask my father. They go in and out, they cook, and they look after the cattle. Meanwhile, they rummage around, they know what we have and don't have, and then they gossip over the whole village.

In the room downstairs, they were holding the wake over my godfather's corpse. He had been placed in a dark coffin, whose inside was lined with white cloth. He was wearing his best suit, and his hands were lying crosswise on his chest. As if he were sleeping! I wasn't afraid of him. Why should I? What really frightened me was to notice he was not breathing. For me, that was the only sign of death.

Sitting, each on a stool, my mother and my aunt were weeping. I was very sorry, more for them than for my godfather, at least he had passed away. My aunt was counting beads on a rosary, and the neighbours who were there followed her. My father was walking about the room restlessly.

Every single hour of the day - a long and stubborn as a mule day - was the same. Hours full of tearful Lord's Prayers, of friendly people who came to express their condolences, with careless hands and the weariness of ploughing drawn on their faces. They were future corpses. "Do whatever you want people to do for you," as the saying goes. You never know who the next one will be. Death neither warns nor chooses. Let whoever falls fall, and so long! My godfather, nobody else but him, who sometimes seemed to be a wise man, used to tell me we start dying the same day we come into this world, and we are a bit closer to death with every day, with every hour… What dreadful things he said!

At nightfall more people came. Carmela de Lois, who attends every wake, told her beads. After dinner, I was told to go to bed, but I didn't want to. I preferred to stay there. I was afraid; afraid of going alone to my room. My godmother had told me dead people appear. They didn't get me to go upstairs. I sat down in a corner by the hearth and there, scared and shivering like a leaf, I remained.

Little by little, almost all of them came to the kitchen. After eating and drinking a lot, they stayed there, sitting around the kneading trough, with their elbows on its lid. There were young men and women who pinch each other cunningly. Somebody brought out a pack of cards, and they started to play all sorts of games you can imagine. When they got bored with the cards, they took to telling stories. They laughed their heads off. They were the same people who had been snivelling and praying in the afternoon. I do not understand people's deceitfulness. How I wish I were a grown-up! I didn't perfectly understand some of the tales either. Hearing their laughter and hubbub, I slowly dropped off to sleep on the stool.

I dreamt of my godfather. He had a very small soul, as white as a snowflake, which flew away from his mouth. I could also fly and followed it. Whenever the soul stopped, I stopped. First, on the granary; then, at the vegetable garden, on the top of an ash tree, at O Castro. We flew and flew night and day among clouds and airplanes till, bang! The snowflake disappeared. I lost my wings and took a dive. From up there I could see the diminished village, the river – which now seemed a little brook-, the farmland. I was sure I was going to smash, but the floor moved and moved away. Until I heard stiff and painful cries…

Frightened, I woke up. I was in my bed. Somebody had taken me there. The sunshine got in through the slots in the shutter. Those cries of my aunt and mum were saying goodbye to my godfather's corpse. Up from the window I could see many people. Neighbours in their best clothes, going to the funeral!

"Dingdong…dingdong", the bell of the church was calling; it was always calling: feast-days, fire, death…

Just like the day before, I went on thinking, surrounded by the loneliness in my bedroom. I thought about people's ease, about how eagerly they fight to earn money, to buy estates, how they go hungry today so that they can eat their fill tomorrow, and maybe that tomorrow never comes, or it takes them by surprise in their graves, feeding worms.

Men are said to fall like flies in wars. Shrapnel tears them to pieces. That's enough to make your hair stand on end, and many people don't realize we also fall in the village. We don't fight against soldiers; we struggle to overcome the hardships of life and the pains in our bodies. Struggling, we die. Not at one sitting like in wars, but there are too many graves in the churchyard. When grass grows around a tombstone, the gravedigger's hoe moves another one.

If only I could understand things! Or even talk about them, tell other people about my thoughts. However, I have already done that and they have laughed at me. And it hurts me. It hurts me to see people walk about the world just like cows and donkeys do: only searching for a feeding trough.

MY FRIEND

MY GODFATHER was not like anybody else. I haven't met a man you could compare him with yet. Everybody chatters about the same things or keeps quiet about the same things. My godfather was different. I can almost see him: sitting on his stool, by the fire, he whistles, he thinks, he draws in the ashes with his stick. He gets cross with nobody. If someone tells him something he doesn't like, he almost always answers back with a light smile, and that's the end of it. It must be for this reason that one day I heard him saying,

"Sometimes, the best way to explain something is to keep quiet."

But whenever he turned to speak, he became a chatterbox. He preached better than a priest. I didn't understand many of the things he used to say, but I longed to hear him. It was, how should I know!... as if a woollen arm on your shoulders pulled you up and you flew far, far away.

One Sunday afternoon, instead of wasting my time, I sat down by him in the kitchen. I asked him about all the things under the sun.

"How do stars die, godfather? Where do roads end? Who laid stones on the riverbed?"

There was nothing he didn't know.

"What is a friend?" I also asked him.

And he lectured me in such a way that I still remember many of the things he said. A whole afternoon talking about friendship!

"A friend is the best thing in the world, if he is true."

"Friends are worthier than money."

"A friend gives you everything and wants nothing; he dies for you if necessary."

After listening to him, I realized I missed not having a friend. It was not easy to find one, my godfather used to say, because most of them are said to be false. At school, I'd got on well with them all since I arrived there. However, when the teacher was dismissed, and Eladia came, and I was the brightest student in class, they took to scowling at me. Like true enemies! They were furious because I could read and write better than anybody else. If they could only imagine what happened to me with Eladia and why I studied! That's how things are: I feel things I can tell nobody. I have to put up with them. All by myself, like when I had the chickenpox and measles! It's even worse because I have to keep quiet!

People at home can or can't be your friends. Being your mother or father has nothing to do with being your friend, I guess. Don Leopoldo is said to be his children's friend; and they talk straightforwardly about everything under the sun. But things are not like that in the village. Those are customs from the city.

After my godfather had delivered that lesson, I spent a long time suffering for not having a friend, until the deed at the dam took place.

It was a December afternoon. It was raining hard and the river began to rise. My godmother told me to fetch the wringer, which was on the river dam. And so I did. I ran as fast as I could, but when I grabbed it, one of my clogs slipped and I fell down into the muddy water. The river flow dragged me down the dam, faster and faster. I did not lose consciousness, but I almost did. All of a sudden, I felt someone pulling up one of my legs, and shortly after, I was at the riverside. Lelo de Cidre had saved me. I gave him a willing hug. But for him, I would have drowned.

"You must care about friends, as you care about a brood," my godfather had said.

I, sure as I was Lelo was a real friend, turned to love him and show him my esteem.

Lelo was very poor. Like me, he was a tenant's son. But he had the advantage of not thinking about things. He used to sing and laugh even when he had nothing to eat or wear. He reminds me of the story the Jew tells, the story of the happy man who hadn't a rag to his back.

In a beautiful small tin box - I hadn't bought the clay chest at that time - I kept my little savings. Several pesetas I had gathered. Who had given them to me? A helpful boy always gets something; for looking after the agricultural technician, for taking the sirloin to the priest and other gentlemen when the pig was killed.

I went to Lelo's house to give him my money box, as well as a white belt my uncle Braulio had brought me from Africa.

"I want nothing from you," he told me.

"But for you, I wouldn't be alive. You saved my life. I can't swim and I would have crashed into the grid of the mill."

"Yes, that's right. But you're not expected to pay for that."

"There is no money enough to pay for that," I told him. "I haven't come here to pay off a debt; I bring you a present."

After chatting for a long time, he accepted my belt.

"I want to be your friend, Lelo."

"We are already friends."

"I want to spend the time together, to talk about our things…"

"So far as I'm concerned, I agree," he told me.

And I did have a friend. A true friend! We got on well together. Every day we used to imagine different fantasies that would happen when we were grown up. Lelo wanted to learn music and play the tuba or the trumpet. He was already practising with the flute, and he was quite good at it. He had also taken it into his head to be a sailor. He had never seen a boat or the sea, but his father had done his military service in O Ferrol and was always talking about tides and winds. I longed to be a schoolteacher or a smith, at least. But I would also like to fly. To fly a plane all over the world, to fly over clouds!

We used to build birdcages, to leave sets of hooks in the river, to fish trout, and there was no rabbit hole without a noose of wire made by us. In the village, we were called "the rascals." Manolito, the landlord's son, was in a rage.

When harvest came, we went to pick ergot. We went over all the fields. As long as we didn't step on the rye, the owners didn't care if we got the crow's corn. After soaking, it weighed three pounds. We also made a wooden rake, to sell at

San Martiño fair, and some windmills. Lelo kept the money we earned, in a box with a lock.

We spent nothing on trifles. Our savings were rising. And they got even higher with the plum of the fox a hunter, a friend of Lelo´s father, sold us. It was a big, plump fox. We hung it from a stick and shouldered it from door to door, as people usually do.

"Hi! Is there anybody in? Do you give something for the fox?"

"Where did you trap it?"

"Over there, at the foot of O Castro."

People would doubt, but as they knew we were always messing about with snares and traps, they ended by giving us some eggs or money. And when the fox started to stink, we gave it to some boys from the other side of the river, who played the same trick on their neighbours.

I got Lelo used to musing about things. Soon after, he seemed to be another boy. Those who don't think don't deserve to be human beings, I guess. We used to talk about very grave matters. Grown-ups´ matters! We agreed there are rich and poor people in the world and things should not be like that. I convinced him it was necessary to learn a lot of things, and I taught him to count and to write better.

Learning things, growing up, courting girls, tubas, trumpets, anvils, ships, aeroplanes, seas, clouds… Every day we would talk about our longings. Like two friends who love each other.

But everything comes to an end. It's clear I can't be happy for a long time. Lelo´s parents decided to go to America.

"I knew nothing about it, Balbino, otherwise I would have told it to you. They arranged our papers secretively."

"It's all over now," I told him. "There is nothing much to do about it. You go away and that's the end of it."

I went to see him off at the bus stop. We spoke hastily. We talked about everything. I even told him about what had happened to me with Eladia. I gave him my secret as a present. At the same time, I learnt he had gone through something like that with the blacksmith's daughter. We had kept hold of only these two things.

"Write to me," I told him. "At least, send me a letter. Do not do like Miguel. Tell me how America is like. Tell me if it's true there are Indians and very long snakes."

Lelo was in tears.

"Don't weep. A man is not a sheep!" But my cheeks also got wet.

As long as I lived in my village, I didn't meet a friend like Lelo. A true friend, who had saved me from drowning at the dam! "Friends are worth more than money." My godfather was right. My godfather was a wise man.

A SEXTON

AND SO IT WAS. When we are down on our luck, we say, "You never know what's waiting for you," and we should say the same when we are in luck. Because I couldn't really compare with Manolito, not even with Pepe das Chouzas, who has a watch and has gone to Santiago twice; but for me, unlucky as I am, that was more than enough.

One night we heard the dog bark. Someone knocked at the door. It was Xaquín do Relanzo. He came in, sat down, and my father brought a jar of wine. They talked about everything under the sun. It was getting late and we were all nodding. Then, Xaquín stood up and, at last, he said what he had come for.

"Well. The boy is what I'm really interested in."

"To exploit him?" My clumsy aunt said, laughing.

"I am serious. You already know I have to take charge of Saint Roque´s Day festivities and all the church chores are my affair: to toll the bells, to help in funerals and anniversaries, to take care of the sacred figures. I neither have time for, nor feel like doing those things. So I thought Balbino, if I paid him the usual wages, might want to do them for me."

"I do want," I hastened to say.

My family raised no objections. And so I became a sexton. I was said to have been the youngest sexton ever in the parish.

Every year there is a new person in charge. My father said the priest used to auction off, at the altar, the right to be that person, and the winner was the bidder who offered more pounds of wax. There had been some troubles, and they had decided that the newly-weds should take it up.

They agreed that, in the beginning, Xaquín had to give me the suit I chose and paid me twenty pesos [7] at the end of the year. And so he did. He took me to the tailor's in Morás, and the first Sunday I went to church, I put on the suit for the first time. I had never had such a good suit.

"Boy, you are looking very smart!"

---

[7] Peso (pl. pesos) a 5 peseta coin

"It's perfectly clear his clothes are half of the boy's looks."

"I bet my life this busybody already courts girls."

Everybody told me something. I laughed and kept quiet. It was as if overnight I had become another person. Such praises came from people who used to see me in rags daily. What an incredible thing clothes are! They judge you by appearances.

My Sunday chore was to sweep clean, to fill up the holy water font, to light and put on the candles, to collect donations, and to toll the bells. My father, who had been a deacon when he was young, taught me many of the things I didn't know. I learnt quickly. When the agricultural technician's sister died, I tolled her death, and I did it well. Then, I tolled the funeral bell for two days, as usual, until they buried her. A lot of priests came along, and at the end I helped them to eat the snacks in the vestry. I gobbled cheese, white bread, and sausages. Besides, they gave me two pesos.

I took a liking to the job, even when sometimes I got cross. With the two pesos, I bought a big cowbell, which I still have. It was my money, but even so, I was smacked at home when they knew I had spent it. I do not understand why, if I had earned it, I couldn't please myself. For my parents I am a boy, and I don't know how to invest money. I almost told them they don't either, because they have bought a sick calf, rotten cabbages, a shabby rope... But I didn't breathe a word. They usually hit the roof and make me keep quiet with a punch. They are older and wiser. I'm a boy, a nobody. Someday I'll grow up.

Whenever I tolled the bell, I tried to pull on the rope or the clapper forcefully. I wanted everybody to hear it: in houses, fields, and moors. They had to remember me willy-nilly. Every peal was like a yell, a deafening call that spread: Here I am!

I'm given to ponder, and whenever I was in the church, among sacred figures and clothes, I would think a lot. I mused on Saint Roque, who would be better with a doctor anointing him with ointment than with a dog licking his wound; and I was uneasy when I saw a smart Saint James riding a horse, killing Moors. One doesn't expect to see a saint do such a thing, I guess. At least, he could dismount and fight them man-to-man. And when I looked at the angels' faces, so nice, so pretty, I was sorry they were neither boys nor girls.

At anniversaries, I had to array the catafalque. That oddness was enough to make my hair stand on end. First of all, I laid down a very heavy box, which made me groan when I took it out from the vestry, and then smaller and smaller ones. The one on the top looked like an upside-down hopper, with a cross on its shorter side. "El fin del cuerpo aquí lo tenéis y el del alma según obréis.[8]" "Como me ves te verás.[9]" These, among others, were the words written around the boxes. Besides, there were frightening drawings showing skulls and bones.

I thought I would work away in this plum job, but Morulo became the person in charge of Saint Roque's festivities, and his nephew took my place. Good things never last for ever.

Whenever I put on the suit, I remember my old days as a sexton. I miss the church, the catafalque, and the bells. All this may mean nothing for grown-ups or town boys, but I have never had a better thing.

---

[8] "Here is the end of the body, and that of the soul depends on how you behave." In Spanish in the original.

[9] "As you see me you will see yourself." In Spanish in the original.

Memoirs of a peasant boy

THE OATH

SOME neighbours don't like Serafin, the gravedigger. It may be because, eventually, they will lie down under his hoe. But someone has to do the job, I guess. Even the madman from Quintas knew that when, in the bar, he stammered he was able to take care of himself, except for getting into the cellar.

Serafin doesn't care. They call for him and he goes there. He gets his wage, and that's the end of it. Being lazy, he doesn't speak much. He is rather short and thin –someone has nick-named him "chisel"- and bandy-legged. He usually wears ducks, a corduroy jacket with patches on the elbows, and a big cap with something like a peak.

He is said to have come from the mountains, a long time ago. He lives with his wife, in a house he rented at the foot of O Castro.

He was given a post as a roadman because he was wounded many times in the war. Being a gravedigger is somehow his second job.

I love him. How can people treat him like dirt? He doesn't speak badly of anybody and doesn't sin either.

Without my family knowing it, I have gone to talk to him in the churchyard when there was a funeral. I liked to see him working. He used to lay his jacket on the wall, roll up his sleeves, and start to dig. First of all, he loosed the soil with a hoe and then took it out with a spade.

The last time I saw him was when Aunt Engracia da Granxa died. It was May. I do remember it because it was the day of my oath. In the cypress tree, blackbirds, whitethroats, starlings, and many other birds were warbling. A stubborn din of all the birds you can imagine and put together! I plodded along, by the wall, squeezing pennyworts. I sat down on a white, marble stone.

"Hi, Balbino! Have you come to see me working?" he said to me.

"Yes, I have."

"I would not expect that. Besides overworking, dammit, digging for a mere pittance, they nickname you and pull faces."

He spat on his hands and went on digging and groaning. I started to spin a ring off a gravestone. Shortly after, he dropped the hoe and sat down by me. That day, he was chatty.

"It is still early! He said, glancing at the shade of the cypress tree on the wall of the church. Another go and I'll finish the hole. Poor Aunt Engracia! You can never say what will become of you. She was the richest person in the parish, while Don Alexandre was still alive. In her house, dammit, the poor ate their fill and the doors were wide open, till things began to go from bad to worse, and her house and goods were finally seized, leaving her to wander the world.

"Had Aunt Engracia really got a lot of money?" I asked him.

"Plenty... but as the saying goes, "whoever lives beyond his income..." When they seized their house Don Alexandre was still alive. He went mad and turned to begging for his bread. It was a pity to see him like that, in rags and smelly. Dammit, how changeable life is! One morning he was found dead in the deep lane. Later we knew he had skidded while walking along an upper path, rolled down, and met his death. He is buried over there, can you see?" he threw a pebble at three fallen gravestones.

"What about Aunt Engracia? Did she go mad?"

"She didn't even want to beg. She considered it beneath herself. She always kept those lady's manners. Neighbours used to take some things to her hut, otherwise she would have starved."

Serafín lighted a cigarette and glanced, once again, at the shade of the cypress tree. I went on playing with the ring while I was thinking about Aunt Engracia, about madmen, about death...

"What is death?" I asked the gravedigger.

"What nonsense a boy can ask?... What can I say?.. Death is the worst thing a man can go through. Those who kill themselves didn't deserve to be born. All of us are a ladder with three rungs: to be born, to live, to die. And there are no two ways about it, as old people say. We tremble at death because we don't know what is beyond it. When it comes, those who didn't make good use of their lives, those who waste their time "wool-gathering" suffer more. Those who did something useful know they don't just pass away. You are not able to understand such grave matters for the moment. It is even hard for many grown-ups to make it out."

I thought I had grasped everything Serafín had said, but I kept quiet; I let him go on. He liked people listen to him.

"Muse about this," he told me. "The world is a wheel and we make it go round. Everyone pushes according to his own strength. I bury dead people and mend roads. Others write books, build bridges, or rule nations. But some people are useless and they even dare to pull to pieces whatever is already done. At the end, they must regret it, but it will already be too late. If, beforehand, we knew the day of our death, how deeply our care for the other would be! How deeply we would love life! I learnt all these things in the war. Imagine, the day before your last journey: clasping everybody to your heart; glancing at the sun, fields, trees; striding along the roads you have once walked; taking your leave; doing in those few hours something our work would be engraved on, so the living would remember us."

He talked endlessly as if he were in a pulpit, waving his arms. Once again, he glanced at the shade of the cypress tree on the wall. Suddenly, he stood up, picked up the hoe, and went on working.

"All right," he shouted. "Get closer. Here you are. This is what remains of a man. Look - he showed me a few long bones - these were legs and arms; and here's the head. Worms have taken the flesh. Shit! However, the new well, with its four iron taps, is still pouring water to his neighbours' advantage, thanks to the efforts of Manuel de Rendos, the owner of the bones you are looking at. I buried him nine years ago. Rendos will live as long as the well lasts, no matter that his bones have rotted away."

Serafín stopped talking. He was, I assumed, thinking about Rendos, the man who had built the well. He resumed his digging. He left the bones in a corner in the hole. I went away across the graveyard, pulling up small plants and stones, squeezing pennyworts. The din of the birds in the cypress tree went on. The funeral bell was tolling.

I headed to the fields. Serafín´s words were going with me: they were buzzing deep inside of me as if there was a wasp's nest behind my forehead. Don Alexandre, Aunt Engracia, death, the last day... I swore to do useful things when I grew up - not to die completely when I die. Every day I muse about this, and about the people who waste their time "wool-gathering", as Serafín says. I will fulfil my oath.

THE STONE

THAT was just the beginning. Because things normally come interwoven. Then you start to uncoil the skein till you, little by little, find the end of the thread. Living, with such ramblings, looks like a tangle, a game of billarda. If only we knew everything beforehand! Although I now think I might have done the same thing I did. Or even worse! It's like a stink you can't get rid of. How should I know!..

Manolito was a very mean boy. Everybody said so. I have always walked my way trying not to bump into him, but he used to provoke me. More than once I was tempted to tan his hide, as my grandmother says. I was not able to. He was the landlord's son. I bore it not to upset my father. We, the poor, usually lose. Justice does not take our side. Manolito knew that well. That is why he nicknamed me.

The priest used to tell us at catechism that if we are slapped on the face, we have to turn the other cheek; but it seems to me that's not fair. Someday, we have to stand up to it.

That afternoon, I was coming back home from the meadow. I had gone there to divert the water in the drains. I had been digging round the potatoes; I had an ache in my kidneys. My throat was too dry and my eyes were stubbornly sore. Thirst, weariness, anguish at seeing that life is not the same for all children.

When I went by the landlord's house, the hoe on my shoulder, I saw Manolito on the veranda; he was playing hide-and-seek with the two boys of Don Leopoldo, the doctor. Don Leopoldo lives in Santiago, but he likes fish so much that in summer he spends some time in the village. He stays at the nabob's house. He is always by the house fishing for rainbow trout, brown trout, and speckled chars. People love him. He is a nice person. And so are Doña Isaura and their children, though Manolito has spoiled them a bit.

"¿Véis aquel harapiento? Es hijo de nuestro casero. Un cagardas. Un...[9]"

I stopped and stared at him. I didn't hear the other words he said to his mates. I didn't want to hear them. I started to tremble like a leaf; not with fear, with rage.

---

[9] Can you see that boy in rags? He is our tenant's son. He is a coward. A... In Spanish in the original.

"Let's go for him," said the naughty boy. They came down and strode up the road. Manolito, shouting, led the group. I could even hear some of the outrages coming from his mouth. I bent down, picked up a stone, and flung it at him. The stone was like a blackbird, flying. I got a bull's-eye, and Manolito fell headlong. I saw his face bleeding. Don Leopoldo´s children surrounded him. I took to my heels. It was as if I was waking up from a nightmare. I could not run faster. The dryness in my throat turned into sourness, and I felt cold on my forehead. The sun seemed to me like a bloody wheel as it went in behind the hill. A young woman was fetching water; I almost ran into her. A child, sitting by a door, was crying. Far off, a car was going away creaking.

It was getting dark. I strode away. Tired because I had been working all day, I felt like fleeing that way. I was afraid. The Brandamo road was dark. The crickets were chirping. Some bats flew over my cap. Night, with its fears, its barn owls and ghosts, was falling. My heart was beating hard. Again and again I looked back. I heard shouts and galloping horses behind me. They might have followed me, but I saw nobody.

Aunt Estrela is my mum's cousin. I got used to calling her aunt. She has lived alone, in Brandamo, since her husband died in the war.

"Who is there?" She shouted from the kitchen, after hearing the doorknocker.

"It's me, aunt. It's Balbino."

She was astonished. I told her about what had happened to me with Manolito, about his provocations, and about the stone.

"Did you hurt him badly?" She asked, weeping.

"I don't know. He tumbled down on the road. He might have died."

"Shut up! Don't say that! God forbid!"

I was sorry for my aunt, for my family, for Manolito, even for myself. I felt myself to be a criminal.

That night I did not sleep well. I dreamt of Manolito again and again. At times, I dreamt I had crushed his eyes with the stone. At times, I dreamt he had become mute, and he had died. His soul, laughing, looked at me from the veranda. He was no longer a quarrelsome boy, but a heaven's angel, with wings as white as snow and a gleaming face. I, standing by his side, with my patches and muddy clogs, was filthy. And I was even filthier because now there was a killer spirit deep inside of me. That night seemed very long to me. As if it was a series of added nights! I wanted to go away. To flee to a place nobody knew me. And I also wished to die. I raised my hands and prayed. I had never liked praying, and now I was doing it for Manolito. Just imagine!

In the morning, the news was known in Brandamo. People were talking about it: a stone the tenant's son flung at him killed the landlord's son. His forehead was cracked.

"I'll take you home right now," said Aunt Estrela.

She took me by the hand and started to walk. I let myself go. I was bewildered. I didn't care two hoots! I knew for sure my father was going to thrash me, but I was not afraid. I almost wished the punishment.

As I was getting into the village, everybody made a wry face. At least, so it seemed to me. I didn't raise my eyes from the ground. I was terribly ashamed.

At home, my mother, godmother, and Aunt Carme scolded me as harshly as they could. They told me we were down and out because the landlord would evict us and we should have to wander the world. Besides paying for Manolito´s medical charges, of course!

My father came from the moor with a small sickle in his hand. He saw me and kept quiet. But at once, he hinted that I ought to follow him. I realized we were heading to the landlord's house. As we walked along the road, we didn't utter a word.

There the landlord was, in the yard, surrounded by honeysuckles and walnut trees, sitting on a stone bench. On hearing our steps, he turned round and cast a furious, raging glance at us, which frightened me. Then, with a wicked smile, he handed a folded rope to my father. I do not remember what I thought, and I closed my eyes. My father moaned with every stroke he gave me on the back, on the legs, wherever. He made me bleed. I fell down twice, and twice I stood up quickly. I even felt up to running to the place where that wolf called "Sir" was, and spat in his face. Then I did the same to my father. At that point, I slipped and no longer realized what happened later on. I lost my consciousness.

When I came round, I was at home. On a stool, beside me, my godmother was sitting down. My mother didn't take long to show up. She spoke to me and caressed me softly, but I was a little bit confused, as if my heart was broken, torn to pieces. No longer did I have a pain in my body, but in my soul. It grieved me to see the landlord take half of our harvest, and on top of all that, besides paying for Manolito's medical charges, to be punished under his very nose so that we got on with him.

"Speak to me, my dear. Where does it hurt you?"

"Balbino, don't be stubborn; say something."

But I kept quiet. I turned round towards the wall and kept quiet.

They got out.

I didn't want to have a bite to eat all day. I didn't get up either. I thought they would talk about me at night. After dinner, they always speak about the things that happened during the day. I went close to the wardrobe. There, I put my ear to a hole that a pine knot had left in a board, and I learnt everything.

I learnt we hadn't got enough money to pay for Manolito's affair, which cost three thousand pesetas, and I also learnt the landlord had thought to evict us. They said I was the cause of that mishap and they agreed I should become a servant. In this way, I would learn to "eat the bread the devil had kneaded,"

I did not want to know anything else. I was hungry and all my body ached, but I planned my flight by nighttime.

What time might it have been? I really don't know; it was dark. I took my new suit, my shoes, and my dustcoat. I bundled everything up and got ready to flee. I sluggishly opened the window. I groped my way along the wine arbour towards the road. In a jiffy, I set out.

At daybreak, I had already passed by Alargos and Codeseira. Without thinking it, I was heading towards Loxo, where my sister Celia is working as a servant. I had been there twice, and I even remembered the short cuts.

Celia was surprised at my arrival. I told her the whole story. She also talked to me about things I didn't know.

"When you are a man, you will understand this affair better," she said to me.

She told me she had also run away one morning. Dad happened to see her flirting with a boy by the house and hit both of them with a stick.

"What do you intend to do?" She asked me.

"To work as a servant. If someone wants me," I replied.

And finally, after a lot of comings and goings, I ended up at Landeiro´s. Just imagine! And everything happened because I had hit Manolito with a stone, because I had rebelled once. It's just like when a house is burnt down because a spark has flown into the scuttle.

FATE

SOME PEOPLE SAY that everything that happens to us is already decided beforehand; that we walk along trodden roads. Everybody walks their own way, whether they like it or not, as if an angel, or a witch, led them. I do not believe such a thing.

One day I talked about this to Lelo. We were leaning against the edge of the bridge, gazing at the river. Water striders were walking about on the surface of the water.

"Things happen because they have to, don't they?" he asked me.

I was glad Lelo mused. People who don't use their brains should drown themselves or run wildly on all fours.

"We can manage most of them. And they will come about the way we want them to," I told him. "For instance, it rests with me to jump or not to jump over the bridge right now."

Lelo smiled, proving me right.

I ended up at Landeiro´s because I wanted to. It's true Manolito, and the stone I flung at him, and my parents helped, but, in the end, the idea of running away was mine, and my legs brought me here.

There was a time when I would have been ashamed of being a servant. Today, I am not. If you think twice about it, we are all servants; all of us but those who are owners. People are divided in two classes: those who give orders and those who receive orders.

I have been here only for a while, and how many new things I have gone through!

Landeiro buys and sells cattle. He is a strong, hardworking man, and so he likes other people to work hard too. He scours every single cattle-show. When he talks to you, he shouts as loudly as if he was among calves. But he is not mean. Sometimes he even tells a joke, and when he laughs, a golden tooth shows in his mouth. He is forty-seven years old. He is said to have studied in Santiago to be a priest, but he gave up his schooling to get married. Four months later, his wife died, and some canting old women gossip that it was a Lord's punishment.

He knows I like reading, and he brings me books. I already have eighteen. I don't completely understand some of them. The best of them - I have already read it four times - is one entitled

"Memoirs". The person speaking happens to be a captain, called Smith, who tells everything that he went through in the war. I have even dreamt about him, and I think I would talk to him if I ever bump into him.

I also dreamt about Pachín, about Lelo. Even about Eladia.

Flora and me do most of the work on the farm. At harvest time, there are labourers. Now I feel myself to be another person; stronger, as if I had become a man. My clothes are a bit short for me. Flora has made me almost forget Eladia, though I feel something different for Flora. I feel like hugging her or patting her on the buttocks, as Landeiro sometimes does. One day, on the moor, we started to romp while we were filling the cart with brushwood, and I don't know what happened to me. Peeping at her calves, my eyes were so dazzled and my blood so excited that I started to tremble.

Flora is twenty years old. She has been working as a servant at Landeiro's since she was young. I was told she sleeps with him some nights. People are always gossiping. They also say the master doesn't let her have a boyfriend. If I were older! But I am a boy, and whenever I mention something to her, she laughs at me.

Celia, my sister, comes to see me every month. One day she came into my room and I had to hasten to hide my notebook. My father also turned up three Sundays ago. We didn't speak much. He told me the landlord hadn't evicted them, provided that I never go back to the village. Besides, he has raised our rent. Manolito has already come back home. He can see with both eyes, but the scar will forever be on his forehead. I regretted seeing my father so grave. On other occasions, he had told me tales and funny stories from his youth. But now there was a stone between us. The stone I had flung at the landlord's son. Even so, if he had spoken to me in a different way, I would have begged his pardon for having spat at him and run away from home. But everything remained the same. He told me my godmother has a pain in her kidneys again, that mum and Aunt Carme will come to see me soon.

When he was just leaving, he gave me a folded piece of paper, which he had taken out of the pocket of his jacket. It was a green envelope. I opened it. A letter from Lelo! The first time I ever received a letter. My friend had remembered to write to me. He carried out his promise. He didn't do as Miguel had done.

I felt as if the sun was shining only for me, as if the chirp of birds was resounding in my chest. How many things Lelo told! I also told him a lot of things in my reply. I told him about my flight, about Manolito, about Flora... Finally, I found a place where I could empty out my uneasiness, the anguishes that grieve me.

Now I don't speak to myself. I tell Lelo, my friend, whatever I used to write down in my notebook. And life, as long as mail exists, has another meaning for me.

I will give my notebook to Alberte, Landeiro´s nephew, who studies in Santiago and writes books. He must be a bit crazy. He picked it up one day in my bedroom and he is always asking me for it. He says it is my "Memoirs". That's typical of Alberte... One night we had talked about Captain Smith and his war adventures. But my notebook, though it's worthy for me, can't be compared with it. He swore to show it to no one.

Let him take it away.

www.ingramcontent.com/pod-product-compliance
Ingram Content Group UK Ltd.
Pitfield, Milton Keynes, MK11 3LW, UK
UKHW041404051225
9406UKWH00024B/132